Billy and the Wizard

by Enid Richemont

Illustrated by Daniel Howarth

W

FRANKLIN WATTS
LONDON•SYDNEY

Once there was a
wicked wizard.

He stole people's food.

He took all their
best things.

If anyone complained,
he turned them into frogs.

"I can't bear this!" said Billy's mum. "We should do something."

"I have a plan!" said Billy.

Billy set off for the
wizard's castle.

"Go away or I'll turn you into something nasty!" shouted the wizard.

"Oh, Mr Wizard, you're so clever!" sighed Billy.

"I know," replied the wizard.

13

"You can turn people into frogs," said Billy.

"I can do anything!"
boasted the wizard.

"Can you turn yourself
into something?"
asked Billy.

The wizard turned into a dragon, breathing fire.

"Wow!" said Billy.
"Can you turn
into a horse?"

"Neigh!" replied the wizard.

"But can you turn into something really tiny," said Billy, "like a mouse?"

"Squeak!" replied the wizard.

"I bet you can't turn into something really, really tiny," said Billy, "like a fly?"

"Buzz!" replied the wizard.

Then Billy swatted the fly
with all his might.

"The wicked wizard is gone!" Billy yelled.

Lots of the frogs turned
back into people ...

... and they all had a party to celebrate.

Leapfrog has been specially designed to fit the requirements of the National Literacy Framework. It offers real books for beginning readers by top authors and illustrators. There are 26 Leapfrog stories to choose from:

Rhyming stories are available with Leapfrog Rhyme Time.

* hardback